Smithsonian Prehistoric Zone

Triceratops

by Gerry Bailey
Illustrated by Karen Carr

Crabtree Publishing Company

www.crabtreebooks.com

Crabtree Publishing Company

www.crabtreebooks.com

Author
Gerry Bailey

Illustrator
Karen Carr

Editorial coordinator
Kathy Middleton

Editor
Lynn Peppas

Proofreaders
Reagan Miller
Kathy Middleton

Prepress technician
Samara Parent

Print and production coordinator
Katherine Berti

Copyright © 2010 Palm Publishing LLC and the Smithsonian Institution, Washington DC, 20560 USA
All rights reserved.

Triceratops, originally published as *Triceratops Gets Lost* by Dawn Bentley, Illustrated by Karen Carr
Book copyright © 2003 Trudy Corporation and the Smithsonian Institution, Washington DC 20560.

Library of Congress Cataloging-in-Publication Data

Bailey, Gerry.
  Triceratops / by Gerry Bailey ; illustrated by Karen Carr .
    p. cm. -- (Smithsonian prehistoric zone)
  Includes index.
  ISBN 978-0-7787-1817-8 (pbk. : alk. paper) -- ISBN 978-0-7787-1804-8
(reinforced library binding : alk. paper) -- ISBN 978-1-4271-9708-5
(electronic (pdf))
  1. Triceratops--Juvenile literature. I. Carr, Karen, 1960- , ill. II. Title.

  QE862.O65B347 2011
  567.915'8--dc22
                        2010044033

Library and Archives Canada Cataloguing in Publication

Bailey, Gerry
    Triceratops / by Gerry Bailey ; illustrated by Karen Carr.

(Smithsonian prehistoric zone)
Includes index.
At head of title: Smithsonian Institution.
Issued also in electronic format.
ISBN 978-0-7787-1804-8 (bound).--ISBN 978-0-7787-1817-8 (pbk.)

    1. Triceratops--Juvenile literature. I. Carr, Karen, 1960-
II. Smithsonian Institution III. Title. IV. Series: Bailey,
Gerry. Smithsonian prehistoric zone.

QE862.O65B338 2011   j567.915'8   C2010-906892-0

Crabtree Publishing Company

www.crabtreebooks.com   1-800-387-7650
Copyright © **2011 CRABTREE PUBLISHING COMPANY.**

Published in the United States
Crabtree Publishing
PMB 59051
350 Fifth Avenue, 59th Floor
New York, New York 10118

Published in Canada
Crabtree Publishing
616 Welland Ave.
St. Catharines, Ontario
L2M 5V6

Printed in China/012011/GW   )101014

Dinosaurs

Living things had been around for billions of years before dinosaurs came along. Animal life on Earth started with single-cell **organisms** that lived in the seas. About 380 million years ago, some animals came out of the sea and onto the land. These were the ancestors that would become the mighty dinosaurs.

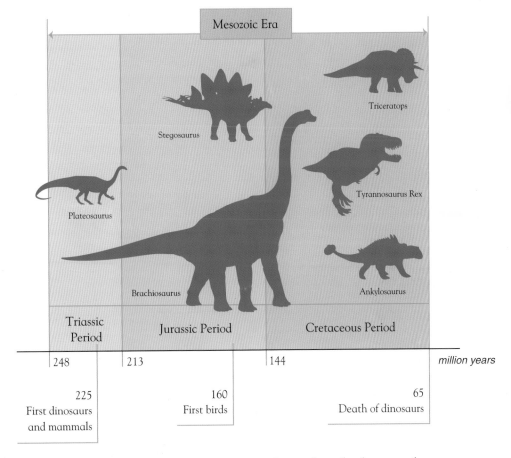

Mesozoic Era

Triceratops

Stegosaurus

Tyrannosaurus Rex

Plateosaurus

Brachiosaurus

Ankylosaurus

Triassic Period	Jurassic Period	Cretaceous Period	
248	213	144	*million years*
225 First dinosaurs and mammals	160 First birds	65 Death of dinosaurs	

The dinosaur era is called the Mesozoic era. It is divided into three parts called the Triassic, Jurassic, and Cretaceous periods. Flowering plants grew for the first time during the Cretaceous period. Plant-eating dinosaurs, such as *Parasaurolophus*, *Triceratops*, and other horned-dinosaurs, roamed the land. Meat-eaters, such as *Tyrannosaurus rex* and *Albertosaurus*, fed on the plant-eaters and other meat-eating reptiles. By the end of the Cretaceous period, dinosaurs (except birds) had been wiped out. No one is sure exactly why.

It was morning. The sun rose over a valley that was rich with trees and other plants. A colorful dragonfly buzzed around flowering shrubs. Trees such as the broad-leafed ginkgo grew alongside

conifers, ferns, and palm-like cycads. This was a forest growing nearly 70 million years ago. Triceratops and his herd had wandered into it to find his favorite plants to eat.

Triceratops suddenly heard a strange thumping
sound coming from the trees. He was curious
to see what was making the sound. He trotted
deeper into the forest. He stopped just in time

to see two dinosaurs fighting for **territory**. They were
called Pachycephalosaurus and they had great bony
caps over their heads. Their heads crashed together
as they charged each other again and again.

7

Triceratops watched for awhile, but these animals were no threat to him and he was hungry. He could see ferns under the branches and these made a tasty meal.

He used his razor-sharp beak to cut through
the stems of the plants. Then his strong jaws
and chopping teeth ground down the tough
plant material before he swallowed it.

Triceratops munched on a clump of delicious ferns. Then he looked for the rest of his herd. It was not in sight. There was not another Triceratops to be seen. He was on his own except for a pair of Avisaurus.

They were known as "opposite birds," and
they perched on a vine nearby. They would
not hurt him. But there were dinosaurs in
the forest that would.

Carefully he made his way into a clearing. He hoped
to find his herd. A sudden, terrible shrieking came
from the sky above. The sound was a warning to him
that several pterosaurs, the largest flying reptiles on

Earth, had spotted him. He had to move quickly. When he glanced up, he saw that the pterosaurs, called azdarchids, were heading for something else on the ground. They were not interested in him.

Triceratops saw the clear stream that ran through the valley up ahead. He needed some water. As he approached he saw frogs, snakes, and turtles along the stream bank. There was a Parasaurolophus drinking too. There was no sign of the herd Triceratops was looking for.

Triceratops **plodded** on. He knew he should not
stop but he was becoming tired and needed to
rest. He found a shady place and closed his eyes.
He was about to fall asleep but was awoken by

animals crying out. The birds were calling
noisily to each other. They had all heard a
loud thudding noise coming their way and
were eager to hide.

The thudding grew louder and was getting closer.
It was the sound of heavy footsteps in the forest.
Then it stopped. The forest was quiet now except
for the slight rustling of leaves.

Triceratops shivered and slowly looked up. Staring down at the horned dinosaur was a pair of flashing eyes. They belonged to a mighty Tyrannosaurus rex— one of the fiercest dinosaurs living at that time.

The great Tyrannosaurus rex looked hungrily at
Triceratops. Its long, sharp teeth were showing as it
opened its jaws. It stood on its **massive** back legs

with its tail stuck out straight behind it to help
balance its huge head and body. It was hungry
and Triceratops would make a tasty meal.

Triceratops was much smaller than Tyrannosaurus rex, but he was not afraid to defend himself. He had three strong, sharp horns on his head that were fearsome weapons against an enemy.

Triceratops watched Tyrannosaurus rex carefully.
He stood his ground and got ready to fight. But
as he did, the ground began to shake and a thick
cloud of dust filled the air.

As the dust cleared, Triceratops saw a line of
horns pointed at the Tyrannosaurus rex. They
belonged to the members of his herd. They had
returned just in time to help him. Slowly the herd

moved toward the great **predator**. He might be
hungry but there was no way Tyrannosaurus rex
could win a battle against so many. The mighty
beast turned and stamped away.

Triceratops was safe. He was back with his herd
and he would stay close to it from now on. He had
learned that one Triceratops on its own was never
far from danger, while a herd of Triceratops was

safe even from giant predators such as
Tyrannosaurus rex. After his long day,
Triceratops felt hungry. He followed the
herd back into the forest to find food.

All about Triceratops

(try-SAIR-uh-tops)

Triceratops lived during the late Cretaceous period between 70 and 65 million years ago. Its name means "three-horned face," as all *Triceratops* had three horns. *Triceratops* had a short neck frill, but it belonged to a group known as the long-frilled group. That is because it had a short nose horn and two larger brow horns like the long-frilled animals. The larger brow horns could grow up to three feet (one meter) long. *Triceratops* would have used its horns to protect itself from enemies or possibly to establish its place in the herd by **jousting** with others of its own kind. Its short neck frill was made up of a solid sheet of bone. It may have been used for show or defense against predators. The frill and horn might have been used for display. It might also have been used as a way for *Triceratops* to **recognize** each other.

There were more *Triceratops* than any other members of its group. It was also the heaviest and largest. It could have weighed up to 12 tons (11 metric tons) and was heavier than a male elephant.

Precambrian Era		570 million years ago		Palaeozoic Era		
Precambrian Period	Cambrian Period	Ordovician Period	Silurian Period	Devonian Period		Carboniferou
				380 First life on land		320 First reptiles

It could have grown up to 30 feet (nine meters) long. Its huge skull could reach almost 10 feet (three meters) long. *Triceratops* walked on four strong, thick legs with hoof-like claws on its feet.

Triceratops was a plant-eater. It had a strong beak that it used to snip through tough plants. It used a set of cheek teeth to help crush the plants.

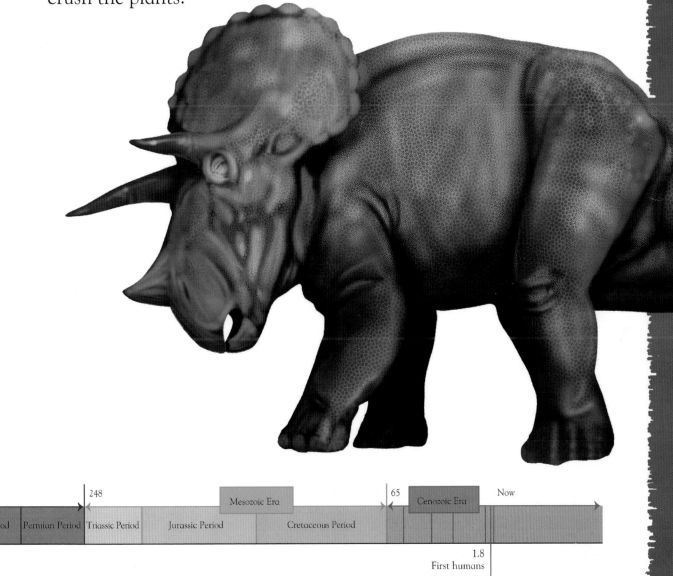

	248			Mesozoic Era		65	Cenozoic Era	Now
eriod	Permian Period	Triassic Period	Jurassic Period		Cretaceous Period			

1.8
First humans

Food

Triceratops was a **herbivore**, or plant-eater. During late Cretaceous times, there was plenty of choice for plant-eating dinosaurs, such as flowering plants.

Triceratops was well equipped to **forage** for the food it needed. At the front of its jaw was a sharp beak, which looked like a parrot's beak. It used this to snip off the tough plant material that it ate. Further back in its cheeks were small teeth for chewing.

Triceratops had powerful jaws that allowed it to eat very tough plants. These included the shrubs and flowering plants that had begun to grow during the late Cretaceous period when Triceratops was living. Herds of Triceratops probably roamed the land, grazing off low-spreading trees and ground vegetation.

sharp beak to snip off tough plant material

small grinding teeth and powerful jaws

Glossary

conifer A tree or shrub with needles and cones

forage To search for food

herbivore An animal that only eats plants

joust To protect or fight using a long object or weapon such as a horn

massive Very large

organism A living thing such as a plant or animal

plod To walk heavily and slowly

predator An animal that hunts other animals for food

recognize To see and know from having seen it before

territory An area of land

Index

Further Reading and Websites

Triceratops Up Close: Horned Dinosaur by Peter Dodson, Ph.D. Bailey Books (2010)

Triceratops and Other Horned Herbivores by David West. Gareth Stevens Publishing (2010)

Websites:

www.smithsonianeducation.org